# Rookie
## of the
# Year

## by Todd Strasser

### BASED UPON THE SCREENPLAY BY SAM HARPER

**BDD**
SPECIAL

*To Lisa, Vanessa and Alexis Acevedo*

Published by The Trumpet Club
1540 Broadway, New York, New York 10036

ISBN: 0-440-40910-1

Produced by Neuwirth and Associates
Printed in the United States of America
September 1993

1 3 5 7 9 10 8 6 4 2

OPM

# one

Standing alone in an alley in the shadow of Wrigley Field, Henry Rowengartner, age twelve, smacked his fist into his mitt and stared up at the ivy-covered walls outside the stadium. Henry was slender and average height for his age. He had black hair, thick eyebrows, and dark expressive eyes that were filled with hope. A tired-looking old man pushed a pretzel cart down the sidewalk past him and smiled. Henry winked back. Above him on the elevated tracks, a Chicago train rumbled past. Henry turned up the volume on his Walkman. Inside the stadium, Henry's beloved Chicago Cubs were playing the San Francisco Giants.

"Here we go, Cubs fans!" Bud Stanky, the voice of the Cubs, cried excitedly over the radio. "Opening Day! The Cubs haven't won a pennant since 1945, but hope springs eternal."

Henry adjusted his yellow-and-black Oak Park

Pirates Little-League uniform. He could hear the crowd inside the stadium cheering wildly. He could imagine Billy Frick, the Cubs' big catcher, crouching at the plate behind the Giants' batter.

"And here comes the first pitch!" Stanky yelled.

Henry imagined himself standing in right field, bracing for the play. *Crack!* Henry winced as he heard the sound of the bat squarely meeting the ball.

"That ball is back . . . back . . ." Stanky shouted. "It's outta here! Well, maybe they'll win the pennant next year, Cubs fans."

Out in the alley, Henry imagined himself inside the stadium, backing against the right-field wall, his glove raised for the catch. Any second now . . . any second now!

There it was! The tiny white dot of the ball sailed high over the Wrigley Field wall and plummeted down toward Henry.

*Smack!* The ball landed in his mitt.

"Rowengartner makes the grab!" Henry cried proudly, holding the ball up for a stadium full of imaginary fans to see.

"C'mon, Henry!" someone yelled, snapping Henry out of his daydream. Down the street he could see his two best friends, George Kavanaugh and Clark Krieger, hurrying down the sidewalk, pushing a baby carriage. George was a heavy boy with short blond hair. Clark was small, with long brown hair parted in the middle. He looked more like he was nine years old than twelve.

Henry ran to catch up to them, and soon all three boys were running along the sidewalk behind the carriage.

"Careful," Clark shouted as they rounded a corner and the baby carriage went up on two wheels. "You're gonna wreck it!"

The boys turned onto Main Street. Ahead they could see Henry's mother step out of her flower shop. Mary Rowengartner was a pretty woman in her mid-thirties, with streaked blond hair pulled back into a ponytail. She raised her hand, and the boys skidded to a stop.

"Henry thinks Coach Edwards is gonna play him today," George said, smirking.

"It could happen," Clark said.

"It's *gonna* happen," Henry said confidently. "David Rosenthal starts Hebrew school this week. Me and Windamere are the only outfielders left."

"Well, it would be great if you got to play," Mrs. Rowengartner said. "But if you don't, I'm going to let you do laundry when you get home."

Henry rolled his eyes. His mother was always giving him chores to do and making it sound as though she was doing him a favor. "You're too kind, Mom," he said sarcastically.

"Have fun," his mother said. The boys started to go, but as Henry passed his mother, she caught him for a second and kissed his head. Henry really wished she wouldn't do that in front of his friends.

"Your mom is so cool," Clark said when Henry caught up.

"She's okay," Henry said with a shrug.

"Hey!" Mrs. Rowengartner called behind them. Henry stopped and turned. His mother wound up like a pitcher and tossed him a tube of sun block. The throw was high and arcing. Henry got under it, ready with his mitt.

*Clack!* Henry missed, and the tube of sun block fell to the ground in front of him.

"Oh, yeah," George laughed. "You're going to get a *lot* of playing time."

Henry was certain he could do better on a real playing field. "Coach Edwards has to put me in," he insisted. "It's either me or Windamere. And Windamere really stinks."

An hour later Henry found himself sitting alone in the dugout at the Little-League field. Down at the end of the dugout, Coach Edwards, a red-faced man with a rotund belly, was yelling instructions to his players in the field. Henry couldn't believe the coach had put Eddie Windamere in right field instead of him. Henry stared out at the scoreboard behind the right-field fence. George and Clark were in charge of keeping score, and it was 10–5 in favor of the Pirates. With that kind of a lead, there was no reason why Coach Edwards couldn't put Henry in.

Henry could hear the parents in the stands yelling as a kid from the Winnetka Braves walked up to the plate.

*"Ha-choo!"* Out in right field, Eddie Windamere sneezed. *"Ha-choo! Ha-choo!"* Between sneezes he tried to wave toward the dugout.

"What the devil's wrong with Windamere?" Coach Edwards asked.

Windamere was sneezing so hard, he was practically doubled over. Greg Teaser, the Pirates' pitcher, was going into his windup.

"Time out!" Coach Edwards called. The Little Leaguers on the field straightened up. The coach turned to Henry. "Get into right field."

Henry jumped off the bench and headed out onto the field. George and Clark started cheering like crazy, but the parents and kids just watched quietly. As Henry jogged out to right field, he saw Becky Fraker sitting in the stands. Becky had long brown hair and big brown eyes. She was in most of Henry's classes at school, and every day he wished he had the nerve to talk to her. She was sitting with Edith Berger, who wore glasses and always had her nose in a book.

Henry got out to right field and nodded proudly at Rick Sherman, the center fielder. Rick looked disgusted. "Just try not to blow it, Rowengartner," he yelled.

Henry nodded. There was no way he was going to blow this. This was his big chance. He slammed his fist into his mitt.

"Okay, Teaser!" He yelled. "Let 'er rip! Throw him the big cheese! Right in the kitchen! Give him the big *stinky cheddar!*"

"Would you shut up?" Rick Sherman muttered.

On the pitcher's mound, Greg Teaser wound up and delivered.

*Crack!* The Winnetka Braves' batter slammed the ball high into the air.

"Heads up, Rowengartner!" Rick shouted.

Henry started backpedaling. The ball looked as though it was going deep.

"Go, Henry!" George screamed.

Henry backed toward the fence. In his mind he could already see the ball heading over the fence. At the last second he would leap up and grab it, saving the home run. He'd be the game's hero!

"I got it! I got it!" Henry shouted as he backed all the way to the fence. He crouched down, ready to leap up and grab the ball . . .

*Thump!* The ball hit the ground ten yards in front of him. Henry heard a loud groan from the stands.

"Get the ball, Rowengartner!" Rick shouted.

The Winnetka player was already rounding first and heading for second. Henry ran toward the ball, tripped, and fell to his knees. His baseball cap fell over his eyes. Suddenly he couldn't see! His teammates were screaming at him, the fans were screaming at him, George and Clark were screaming at him. Henry felt around the grass until he found the ball.

"Throw it, Rowengartner!" Rick screamed.

Henry jumped to his feet and heaved it . . . straight over the scoreboard and into the street.

# two

The game was over. Despite Henry's incredible error, his Pirates had still won. As the crowd started to file out of the stands, Henry hid with his friends in the shadows of the dugout.

"What a nightmare," Henry groaned as he waited for everyone to leave. He couldn't stand the thought of facing anyone.

"You're telling me," George said. "I don't even know if that play was legal."

"Forget about it," Clark said. "When the Pirates look back at this game, they're not gonna remember Henry's throw. They're only gonna remember that they won."

Not far away, Rick Sherman and Greg Teaser were doing wheelies on their BMX bikes in front of a group of girls.

"Look at those guys showing off," George said in disgust. Henry looked over and saw that Becky was one of the girls. As he watched, Rick got off his bike, pulled his baseball cap low over his eyes, spun around as if he was disoriented, and pretended to throw an invisible ball the wrong way.

The kids around him laughed. Feeling stung and humiliated, Henry shook his head. "Let's get out of here," he mumbled.

A little while later Henry and his friends pushed the baby carriage through a hole in the fence as they snuck into Fox Lake Park.

"I don't get it," George said as they started down a dirt path through the woods. "Didn't you say your father was a great baseball player? I mean, before he was lost at sea?"

"George, let it die," Henry said wearily.

"Sorry." George shrugged. "I was just thinking out loud."

They reached a marsh. Pushing the baby carriage through the reeds, they came to a wooden duck blind on the edge of the lake. Lying next to the blind was an old wooden rowboat. The boys stared down at it.

"This lake's gonna be the happening spot this summer," Clark said.

Henry pointed across the lake to a large white clubhouse with flags flying from the roof and lots of sailboats moored at its docks. "But everything that happens is gonna happen across the lake with the club crowd."

"Maybe," said Clark, "but we're going to be the only kids on the lake with our own boat."

"Fully operated by us," George added.

"With absolutely no parental guidance whatsoever," Clark said with a big smile.

His friends' enthusiasm got to Henry. "Yeah," he said. "They'll all be dying to ride with us."

"Exactly!" Clark and George gave each other high fives. Henry turned to the baby carriage.

"Let's unload this baby!" he said happily. The three of them lifted a small, greasy outboard engine from the baby carriage. The boat and engine both needed a lot of work, but once they completed it, Fox Lake would be theirs.

It was almost dinnertime when Henry got home. The houses on his block were small, but neatly kept. Henry pushed open the front door. Inside, his mother was emptying a grocery bag. A large pot of spaghetti sauce was simmering on the stove, and Henry breathed the aroma in deeply and felt his stomach grumble hungrily.

"Hi, Sweetheart," his mother said. "How was the game?"

Henry shrugged.

"Did you get to play?" she asked.

"Yeah. The coach put me in right field." The memory was still painful.

"How'd you do?"

"Let's just say I made the play of the day," Henry said drolly.

His mother sighed. "That bad, huh?"

"I really stink, Mom," Henry admitted.

"Hey, take it easy," she said. "It's just a game. Where's your sense of humor?"

"But I can't even catch a fly ball," Henry said.

"Maybe you're not cut out to be an outfielder," his mother said. "Maybe you should be a pitcher, like your father was."

"Yeah, right." Henry grimaced. "In my dreams." He started out of the kitchen.

"Hey, the laundry," his mother said, pointing to a filled pink plastic laundry basket in the corner. A box of Salvo laundry-detergent tablets lay on top of it.

"How could I forget?" Henry groaned. He took the laundry to the basement. The washing machine was an old, front-loading model. Henry stuck in the laundry, then took a detergent tablet out of the Salvo box. He stared at the round tablet.

"What's this?" Henry said, imitating Bud Stanky. "The Cubs are bringing in the right fielder to pitch!"

Henry walked to the other side of the basement and held a Salvo tablet behind his back. He stared at the washing machine. "The entire season is resting on Rowengartner's shoulders."

Henry wound up and heaved the tablet into the washing machine. "Strike!" he cried gleefully.

He took out another tablet. "Okay, it's the bottom of the ninth. Two out. One on. Full count. Rowengartner takes a long look at the runner on second."

Henry wound up. He was so into his fantasy that he didn't notice Jack Bradfield stepping in front of the washing machine and going into a batting stance, using a toilet plunger as a bat. Jack was Mrs. Rowengartner's boyfriend.

Henry threw.

*Crack!* Jack hit the Salvo tablet so hard it exploded

into a cloud of blue powder. "Cubs lose!" he shouted.

Henry was caught by surprise. "What are you doing down here?"

"Your mom said I could throw these in," Jack said, tossing a pair of jeans into the machine. "So, you want to be a baseball player when you grow up?"

"Who doesn't?" Henry said, shrugging. His mother's latest boyfriend wore wire-rimmed glasses and had brown hair. Henry thought he was a loud, obnoxious show-off.

"Cubs lost again this afternoon," Jack said.

"So what else is new?" Henry replied sadly.

"Sure you can take another summer with your favorite team in the cellar?" Jack asked.

"They'll come around," Henry said. "They just got Chet Steadman back off the disabled list."

"That bum?" Jack chuckled. "He hasn't had any stuff since he had surgery."

Henry slammed the washing-machine door shut. Jack was a jerk. Henry wished his mother had better taste in men.

"Lots of players come back after surgery," Henry said.

"Maybe," Jack said, "but everyone knows that Steadman is afraid to throw hard."

"Maybe when he's rested he'll get his old heat back," Henry said.

"Yeah, sure," Jack said, obviously not believing it. "Look, the Cubs haven't won the World Series since 1908. They're losers, Henry. You should root for the White Sox."

Henry would have eaten dirt first. He turned on the

washing machine and climbed the stairs back to the kitchen. Jack followed him up.

"What were you guys doing down there?" Mary asked as she put a bowl of spaghetti on the table.

"Talking a little baseball," Jack said.

The next thing Henry knew, Jack put his arms around his mother and him and hugged them both. Henry quickly wriggled out of the embrace. He wished Jack would just disappear forever.

"Hey, it's time to go," Jack said. "I just gotta get my jacket."

After Jack left the kitchen, Henry turned to his mother. "You mean, I'm eating alone? You're going out again?"

She nodded.

"What's the occasion this time?" Henry asked.

"Our three-week anniversary," his mother replied.

"Hey, congratulations," Henry said sadly. His mother leaned close to him.

"What have you got against Jack?" she asked in a low voice.

Henry didn't want to hurt her feelings, so he just said, "He's going too fast. I mean, I'm already doing the guy's laundry."

"He's stable, Henry," his mother said. "That's important."

"Well, I think you can do better," Henry said.

"I'm thirty-four now," his mother said, a little wistfully. "I'm not such a great catch."

Henry disagreed. "I think you're a great catch. You're like a five-hundred-pound tuna!"

Mary Rowengartner smiled and rubbed Henry's

head affectionately. A moment later Jack returned to the kitchen.

"The three-week anniversary is called the necklace anniversary, I believe," he said, handing Henry's mother a narrow green box. She opened the box, and her eyes went wide.

"Oh, Jack, thank you!" she gasped, staring down at a thin gold chain.

Henry thought he'd barf when she turned and kissed Jack.

"Okay, let's go," Jack said, holding open the door.

"In bed by eight-thirty," Mary told Henry. "And do your homework."

"And chug a case of brew and jump naked out the window?" Henry asked. It was a private joke between them for whenever she gave him unnecessary advice.

His mother smiled. "That too." She turned and left. Jack looked back at Henry and raised his fist victoriously.

"Go White Sox!" he yelled.

Henry waited until Jack had turned his back, then stuck his tongue out at him. Then he took the bowl of spaghetti and went up to his bedroom.

The walls were covered with Cubs banners, yearbooks, and posters of Henry's favorite players. The biggest poster featured a young-looking Chet Steadman in a pitcher's stance. Henry went to the window and looked down. Jack had just helped Henry's mom into his car. He went around to the driver's side, but before he got into the car, he checked his hair in the reflection of the window.

Henry shook his head sadly. "Oh, Mom, not Jack

Bradfield, please?" he asked quietly. He looked down at the steaming bowl of spaghetti, but he'd lost his appetite. Instead he sat down on his bed and turned on the radio. The Cubs were playing again that night, and he wanted to catch the game.

As Bud Stanky's voice rattled from the radio, Henry pulled out his mitt and ball. The mitt was old and well oiled, and had a piece of tape across the back with ROWENGARTNER written on it. His mother said it had belonged to his father, so Henry cherished it. He tossed the ball into the air and tried to catch it, but the ball bounced off the mitt and fell to the floor. Henry watched the ball roll away. He was hopeless. Truly hopeless.

At school the next day, Henry went through the lunch line with Clark and George, then headed for a table. Rick Sherman and the other good players on the Pirates were having a food fight with the dweebs who wore thick glasses and plaid shirts.

"Duck!" George yelled as a Ding Dong® flew over their heads.

"How come we have to sit at a table in the middle of the food fight?" Clark asked.

"Because it's the only one that's empty," George explained.

Henry knew that wasn't the real reason. Kids like George and Clark and him were always in the middle. They weren't good-looking enough, or good-enough athletes, to hang out with guys like Rick Sherman and Greg Teaser, but they weren't as dorky as the dweebs, either.

Henry sat down with his friends and glanced at a nearby table, where Becky Fraker was sitting. He wished he had the nerve to sit with her. Suddenly Edith Berger came out of the lunch line and walked toward the boys' table.

"Look who's coming, Clark," George teased.

"Shut up!" Clark hissed and looked down at his lunch tray.

"Hi, guys. Mind if I sit here?" Edith asked.

Clark sort of nodded. Edith sat down and started to eat. Henry glanced again at Becky.

"Why don't you go talk to her?" George asked.

"Forget it," Henry said. "We have nothing in common."

"Sure you do," George said. "Her dad has a boat, and we have a boat."

"We don't have a boat," Clark corrected him. "We have some wood in the vague shape of a boat."

"It doesn't matter," Henry said. "Becky doesn't like me."

"Is that true?" George asked Edith.

Edith shook her head. "Cammy Harold told me, and I quote, 'Becky doesn't think Henry's that ugly.'"

George grinned and turned to Henry. "See? You own her."

Henry just rolled his eyes and sighed.

After lunch they went outside to the playground. Becky and her friends were watching Rick and some of the other Pirates play a pickup game of baseball.

"Hey, Rowengartner!" Rick yelled and waved. "Good game yesterday!"

The other ballplayers grinned. Henry winced and

turned to Clark. "I thought you said they'd forget about that play."

"Give it time," Clark replied.

Henry was wondering how much time he'd have to give it when he heard the crack of a bat. Someone yelled, "Hey, heads up!"

Henry looked up in the air and saw a foul ball flying toward them. Becky was watching. So were the guys on the Pirates. Henry had an idea and started to run after the ball.

"What's he doing?" Clark gasped.

"He's gonna try and catch it!" George shouted.

Henry ran as hard as he could to get under the ball. Behind him he could hear the Pirates laughing, but as he got closer to the spot where the ball would land, their laughter quickly died.

"He's actually gonna do it!" someone cried.

A second later Henry reached up and snagged the ball with his bare hand.

"I got it!" he shouted. But another baseball was lying in his path, and Henry stepped on it and went flying.

*Crunch!* Henry landed on his right side. He actually felt the bone in his arm snap, followed by the worst searing pain he'd ever felt.

# three

$H$enry spent the summer with his arm in a cast. It wasn't fun. He couldn't swim or work on the boat. He couldn't play ball. He couldn't even run through a sprinkler without first wrapping the cast in a plastic garbage bag. And if that wasn't bad enough, Jack the Jerk hung around the entire summer, and the Cubs suffered through a terrible losing streak.

Finally the big day came. Mary drove Clark, George, and Henry to the doctor's office. Dr. Kersten cut the cast off Henry's arm and then took some X rays. He studied them in the light while the boys and Henry's mother waited anxiously.

"Well," Dr. Kersten said, "the bone is fine, but the tendons have connected with cartilage in the ulna."

"Is that bad?" Henry's mother asked.

"No, but it is unusual," the doctor said, drawing up a chair and sitting down in front of Henry. "Let's have a look at this arm. Would you move your fingers?"

Henry moved his fingers.

"Fine," said the doctor. "Now raise the arm."

Henry raised his arm.

"Good. Now move it to the side."

He moved his arm to the side.

"Fine. Now rotate from the shoulder slowly."

Henry started to rotate his shoulder. Suddenly his arm snapped down, hitting the doctor in the nose and knocking his glasses off.

"Ow!" Dr. Kersten grabbed his nose.

"Are you all right?" Mrs. Rowengartner gasped.

"I'm really sorry," Henry apologized. "I don't know what happened."

Dr. Kersten let go of his nose. "I think the tendons have healed a little tight," he said. "Give it some time. It'll work itself out. You can go."

Outside on the sidewalk, Mary took an envelope out of her purse and handed it to her son. "Happy cast-off day."

Henry tore open the envelope. His eyes immediately bulged.

"What is it?" Clark asked.

"Oh, nothing." Henry shrugged, pretending to be nonchalant. "Nothing at all . . . *Just three Cubs tickets for noon today!*"

"Gee, thanks, Mrs. R.!" George and Clark gushed.

"Now, you know how to get there," his mother said. "You take the E-line and —"

"Talk to strangers, shoplift, and run naked through the streets?" Henry asked.

"That too," his mother said with a smile.

• • •

At noon the three boys were sitting in the sunny bleacher seats behind center field at Wrigley. The Cubs and the Montreal Expos had just taken their warm-ups, and the game was about to begin.

"Think they have a chance today?" George asked as he ate a hot dog.

"Definitely," Henry said. "Steadman is pitching."

After seven innings, the Cubs were behind, 4–3. Henry had his fingers crossed for Chet Steadman. So far he'd pitched a pretty decent game, but a big Expos' hitter was at the plate.

"Come on, Rocket," Henry whispered. "Throw the heat."

Steadman threw, but the pitch had nothing on it.

*Crack!* The hitter belted a home run off the scoreboard. The ball fell into the empty seats at the back of the bleachers, and the bleacher bums scrambled after it. A big guy wearing a Cubs cap backward got to the ball first and held it up proudly.

"Throw it back! Throw it back!" everyone started chanting.

"Why's he gotta throw it back?" George asked.

"Bleacher rules," Henry explained. "You can't keep a home run that's hit by the other team."

The big guy wound up and heaved, but the ball barely cleared the outfield wall and dribbled onto the grass.

"What an arm!" someone shouted, and the bleacher bums all laughed. Meanwhile, a man in a Cubs uniform stepped out of the dugout and started toward the pitcher's mound. He was joined by the Cubs' catcher.

"Martinella and Frick want to talk it over with Steadman," Henry said.

"Who're Martinella and Frick?" Clark asked.

"Sal Martinella's the Cubs' manager," Henry explained. "Billy Frick's the catcher. They're probably telling him to just get out of the inning so they can pinch-hit him. Come on, guys, we gotta give Steadman some support!"

"Gas him, Steadman!" George shouted as the next batter stepped to the plate.

"Give him the cheese!" Clark yelled.

"Throw him the stinky cheddar, Rocket," Henry cheered.

On the mound, Steadman wound up and delivered.

*Crack!* The ball shot high in the air. Henry knew instantly that it was another home run. He bowed his head. "Back-to-back homers," he groaned.

The ball fell into the bleachers, and once again the bleacher bums, including George and Clark, scrambled after it.

"Got it!" George shouted, coming up with the ball.

"Throw it back! Throw it back!" the bleacher bums shouted.

George started to wind up, then stopped. "Wait a minute," he said. "This game is on cable. The kids from school will see me make a dorky throw."

He tossed the ball to Clark.

"Oh, sure," Clark said bitterly. "Give it to me so I'll get razzed."

"Throw it back! Throw it back!" the bleacher bums shouted.

Clark tossed the ball to Henry, who hadn't thrown a

ball since he'd broken his arm. He decided to give it a try, and threw the ball as hard as he could. Incredibly, the ball streaked across the field like a missile.

*Whap!* Almost four hundred feet away, at home plate, the ball smacked into Billy Frick's glove.

Suddenly the entire stadium went silent. The players, the fans, even the vendors stopped what they were doing and looked around for the person who'd thrown the ball so far so fast. Even the Expo who'd hit the home run stopped rounding the bases and looked.

In the bleachers, Henry looked down at his arm in amazement. George and Clark were staring at him with mouths agape.

"What the heck was that?" one of the bleacher bums asked.

"Uh, sorry," Henry stammered. "I didn't mean it. My tendon's too tight."

"What's your name?" another guy asked.

"It's Henry," George told him.

"Shut up, George," Henry snapped. Now the big guy who'd thrown the last home-run ball back approached them.

"You tryin' to show me up, Henry?" he said, glowering.

"Uh, no, really," Henry replied nervously. Then he turned to Clark and George. "Come on, guys, let's get out of here."

# four

Later, back at Henry's house, they tied a heavy sofa cushion to Clark's chest and put a football helmet on his head for protection. George stood behind him, wearing a cushion and a colander on his head. Clark picked up Henry's mitt and squatted down like a catcher. Across the yard, Henry went into a pitcher's stance, wound up, and delivered another superfastball.

*Whap!* The ball slammed into Clark's glove.

"*Yeow!*" Clark let out a yelp and jumped up, holding his hand. "I can't feel my fingers!" he cried, wringing his hand.

"You almost killed him," George shouted gleefully. "That ball was *howling!* I bet you're throwing two hundred miles per hour!"

"Nobody can throw two hundred miles per hour," Clark corrected him.

"But it's possible he's throwing a hundred miles per hour, right?" George asked.

"Yeah, it's possible," Clark said.

"Let's do it again," Henry said.

"Are you nuts?" Clark asked.

"Hey, come on," George urged him. "You're making history."

"He's making history." Clark pointed at Henry. "I'm losing the feeling in my hand."

Jack's car pulled into the driveway. They could see Mary in the passenger seat through the windshield.

"Hey," George said with a grin. "You gotta show her."

Henry's mother and Jack both got out of the car carrying grocery bags.

"Hi, Honey," Mary called. "How was the game?"

"The Cubs lose again?" Jack asked with a knowing smile.

"Hey, Mom, watch this," Henry said, ignoring Jack.

George pushed Clark back into position.

"Okay, Henry," George shouted. "Let's see the cheese!"

"Yeah," Clark said. "The high, stinky cheddar!"

Henry wound up and delivered. As the ball screamed toward Clark, he dove out of the way.

*Crash!* The ball had flown over the fence and smashed through a neighbor's window. Stunned, both Jack and Henry's mother dropped their grocery bags.

"So what do you think?" George asked with a grin.

"I think I'm calling that doctor," Henry's mother said.

● ● ●

They waited in the living room while Mrs. Rowengartner spoke to Dr. Kersten.

"What'd he say?" Henry asked when she got off the phone.

"He said there's nothing wrong with your arm," Mary said.

"You told him about the fastball?" Jack asked.

"Yes," Mary said. "He said maybe Henry should try out for the Cubs. I think he was joking."

The idea seemed crazy, but Henry couldn't help smiling.

"I think he's right," Clark said. "With the Cubs' losing record, why not give Henry a tryout?"

"Imagine trying out for the Cubs," Henry said. "Wouldn't that be intense?"

"Totally intense," George said.

Jack had been lost in thought. Now he got up.

"Where are you going?" Mary asked.

"Uh, I'm going to make a phone call," Jack replied.


The next afternoon, Henry was in the basement, doing laundry again. This time he was balling up dirty socks and heaving them into the open washing machine. Clark and George were also in the basement, rummaging around.

"Hey, look," George said, stopping near a wooden crate. "This would be perfect for the cabin."

"The boat's six feet long," Clark said. "Where are we gonna put a cabin?"

"Okay, it'll be a little cabin," George allowed.

"Hey, Henry," Clark said, "would you please tell George we're not having a cabin?"

Henry hardly heard them — he was having too much fun hurling socks.

"*Henry!*" George and Clark shouted together.

Henry looked up. "Huh?"

"We're trying to make an important boat decision here," Clark explained.

The doorbell rang before Henry could reply. "I'll be right back," he said, heading up the stairs.

Henry jogged through the living room and opened the front door. His jaw nearly dropped to the floor. It was Sal Martinella, the Cubs' manager! On the street behind him was a long, black limousine.

"Hello, son," Martinella said. "I'm looking for Henry Rulenfurter."

"Rowengartner?" Henry managed to gasp.

"Yeah, is he here?" the manager asked.

"I'm Henry."

Martinella scowled. "I must be looking for your father."

"I don't have a father," Henry said.

A second later Jack came running up behind them.

"Hey, sorry I'm late," he gasped, shaking Martinella's hand. "You must be Sal Martinella. I'm Jack Bradfield, and I'm a huge Cubs fan."

Henry rolled his eyes in disgust as Jack patted him on the shoulder.

"This is Henry," Jack said, "the next Nolan Ryan."

Martinella stared from Jack to Henry in disbelief. "Sure, and I'm King Tut's monkey." He turned around and started walking back toward the limo.

"Wait!" Jack shouted. "I talked to Mr. Fischer!"

Meanwhile, George and Clark had come upstairs looking for Henry.

"Hey," Clark said when he spotted the limo. "What's going on?"

"I'm not sure," Henry said.

Down by the curb, Martinella was leaning into the window of the limo, having an argument with a man inside, who was wearing sunglasses and a dark suit.

"You brought me all the way out here to look at a twelve-year-old?" Martinella was shouting at the man.

"That's right," the man in the limo said. "Is he coming?"

"No!" Martinella snapped. "He's not coming, because I'm not looking at him."

"Go get him," the man in the limo said calmly.

"Never!" Martinella shouted angrily. "This is an insult!"

Back in the doorway, Jack took Henry by the arm and started down the front steps.

"What's going on?" Henry asked.

"You said you wanted a tryout with the Cubs, right?" Jack asked.

"Well, yeah," Henry said, "but I never thought —"

"You're trying out for the Cubs!" George gasped.

"Incredible!" Clark cried.

"It's a dream come true," Jack said with a wink. "Now, do it."

Henry stared at the limo, where Martinella was still

arguing with the guy in the suit. The idea was crazy, but now Henry was pumped.

"Do it, Henry!" Clark shouted. "Throw him the cheese!"

"The high, stinky cheddar!" George shouted, tossing him an apple from the kitchen.

"Hey, Mr. Martinella," Henry yelled. The Cubs' manager looked up.

Henry heaved the apple.

*Splat!* It smashed into a stop sign and instantly turned into applesauce.

"Holy Christmas!" Martinella gasped.

"How about them apples?" Jack asked with a grin.

George and Clark ran up to Henry.

"Nice pitch," Clark said.

"And under pressure, too," added George.

"I was aiming for the mailbox," Henry admitted with a shrug.

Martinella pulled open the door to the limo. "Come on, everyone," he said. "We gotta find us a field."

They drove over to the field where Henry played Little League. Martinella went to the trunk of the limo and got out some baseballs and a speed gun. He gave the balls to Henry and told him to go over to the pitching mound. Martinella went behind the backstop and held up the speed gun.

"Okay, kid, do it!" he shouted.

*Clang! Clang! Clang! Clang!* Henry threw four pitches against the backstop. By the time he was finished, he'd left a sizeable dent in the fencing. Martinella shook his head in wonder.

"I don't believe this," he muttered. "The slowest pitch was a hundred and four miles an hour."

Henry came off the mound. He noticed that Jack and Mr. Fischer, the man with sunglasses, were talking quietly. Mr. Fischer gave Jack some papers, and they shook hands. Then Mr. Fischer turned to Martinella.

"So what do you think?" he asked.

"He's good," Martinella said. "Real good."

Fischer smiled and turned to Henry. "How'd you like to pitch for the Chicago Cubs, kid?"

Henry was flabbergasted. Clark and George grabbed each other and started dancing around crazily.

"Well?" Fischer asked.

"Uh, I really appreciate the offer, sir," Henry managed to reply. "But I have to talk to my mother first."

That night Henry's mother sat on the living-room couch, looking at the contracts Jack wanted her to sign. Mary looked up and shook her head.

"I don't even know what any of this means," she said.

"It's a standard rookie contract," Jack tried to explain. "It's for one season, and it means Henry is going to get the opportunity of a lifetime."

Henry couldn't hide his eagerness. It really was a dream come true! Not to mention everything he'd ever wanted. "C'mon, Mom, please?"

"I thought it would make you happy to see Henry so excited," Jack said.

But Mary was more upset than happy. "How could you do this without asking me?"

Jack slid down onto the couch beside her and put

his arm around her shoulders. "Nothing's done yet, Mary. But don't worry, I'll handle everything. All you have to do is sign."

He tried to hand Henry's mother a pen, but Mary pushed it away.

"Henry's only twelve years old," she said, a little sadly.

"Actually, he's almost thirteen," Jack said.

Mary glared at him. "I know when my son's birthday is! He's too young to be hanging around with a bunch of foulmouthed, beer-guzzling, overpaid baseball players."

Jack and Henry glanced at each other.

"Tell you what," Jack said, getting up from the couch. "Why don't we sleep on it?"

"Good idea," Mary said, and then quickly added, "Good night, Jack."

Jack headed for the front door, but as he pulled it open, he looked back at Henry and Mary. "Don't forget," he said, "this is the opportunity of a lifetime."

Jack went out and closed the door behind him. Henry sat down next to his mother on the couch. He had to figure out a way to get his mom to let him sign with the Cubs.

"Mom," he said, "if you let me do this, I promise I'll never ask for anything again for as long as I live."

"We'll see," Mary replied.

Henry couldn't bear the thought of her saying no. "Listen," he said, "Mr. Fischer said I was the Cubs' hope for the future."

Mary put her arms around Henry and hugged him. "You're *my* hope for the future, too," she said, and kissed him.

• • •

Henry hardly slept that night. The next morning he got up early and set the kitchen table. He got some flowers from the garden and put them in a vase, then placed the contract and a pen beside them. Then he made pancakes for breakfast. A little while later Mary trudged into the kitchen, wearing her robe. Her hair was a mess, and she had dark rings under her eyes. Henry could tell that she'd gotten even less sleep than he.

"Good morning, Mom," Henry said with a smile.

"Hmmm," Mary grunted and sat down at the table. Henry wasn't even certain she'd noticed that he'd set it.

"Oh, boy, do I smell pancakes?" he asked, setting a plate of pancakes before her. "And how about some bacon, er, kind of?"

The bacon had come out a little well done. Actually, it was charred almost black. Mary stared up at him. Henry knew the verdict was coming.

"I have to work," she said. "I can't be chauffeuring you around all the time."

Henry's eyes went wide, and his heart filled with joy. "You won't!" he gasped. "I swear!"

"You'll have to do all your homework," his mother said.

"Agreed," said Henry.

"If your grades start to slip, the deal's off," his mother said.

"They won't, I promise," Henry assured her.

"And you must come home immediately after games," Mary said.

"I must!" Henry repeated. "Because I'll have all that homework!"

"And there's one more thing," his mother said. Henry suddenly felt a chill. She'd covered everything important. Did she have one last stipulation that would be the deal-breaker?

"If anything happens to you, Henry Rowengartner," his mother said. "I'll kill you."

"Great!" Henry grinned. His mother picked up the pen and signed the contract. Henry stared at the papers in amazement. It was done! He had just become the youngest major-league pitcher in history!

Later that day a long, black limousine stopped in front of their house. Mr. Fischer got out and told Henry and his mother that he was taking them to Wrigley Field for a press conference.

Jack met them at the stadium and gave Mary a big kiss.

"You did the right thing," he said happily.

"We'll see about that," Henry's mother replied uncertainly.

Mr. Fischer led them down a hall to the press room. He pushed open the door. The room was filled with newspaper reporters and television crews. Up in front, a white-haired man stood at a podium, bathed in bright camera lights, speaking into a bunch of microphones.

Mary immediately turned to Jack. "You didn't tell me it was going to be such a zoo," she whispered, putting her arm protectively around Henry's shoulders.

"I didn't know," Jack said innocently. "But stop worrying. It's just part of the game."

"He's right, Mom," Henry said eagerly. "It's gonna be great!" Mary gave him a doubtful look. Henry was still worried that she might change her mind.

Now Mr. Fischer turned to them. "I've got Pepsi®, Kellogg's®, and Reebok® foaming at the mouth for a piece of this kid."

Henry's mother stared at him. "Which piece?" she asked.

Mr. Fischer laughed. Henry's mother laughed too, but Henry could tell she was faking it. Henry watched as the smile faded from Mr. Fischer's lips. He pulled Jack to the side and whispered urgently to him. Henry couldn't hear everything, but he thought he heard Mr. Fischer ask Jack if Mary was going to be a problem. Jack replied that he could handle her.

Now the man at the podium began to speak again. "Good afternoon, ladies and gentlemen. As you know, I'm Bob Carson, the owner of the Cubs. I'm not much on gimmicks, but I think we've got something special here."

He waved to the back of the room for Henry and the others to come forward. "Please say hello to the little man with a big-league gun. Henry! Come up here and meet the press!"

Henry and the others walked up to the front. Mr. Carson pulled up a footstool so Henry could stand at the podium and speak into the microphone. Henry had to squint into the bright camera lights. His mother stood on his left, and Jack stood on his right.

A reporter in the audience raised his hand. "I know

the lady is Henry's mother," he said, "but who's the gentleman?"

"Jack Bradfield," Jack said. "I'm Henry's agent."

Henry and his mother looked at each other in surprise. They'd never even talked about that. But they couldn't say anything in front of the press. Another reporter raised his hand.

"We've been told that since you broke your arm, you can throw the ball over a hundred miles an hour. The question is, can you pitch?"

"Well, uh ... " Henry looked over at his mother. "My dad used to play."

"Semipro? Pro?" a reporter asked.

"I'm not sure," Henry said. "But he was a pitcher."

The crowd of reporters laughed, although Henry wasn't sure why.

"What about you, Henry?" a female reporter asked. "Do you have any pitching experience?"

"Yeah, Little League," Henry said. "I play right field for the Oak Park Pirates, kind of."

The reporters turned their questions to Mr. Carson. "When are you going to pitch the kid?"

"He'll be in uniform tomorrow," the Cubs' owner said. "We want him ready for our West Coast swing next week."

"Is he a starter?"

"We're going to use him as a reliever," Mr. Carson said.

As Carson spoke, Henry closed his eyes and imagined the people he knew watching him on television. He could just picture Rick Sherman and Greg Teaser going berserk. He could see Coach Edwards having a heart attack. Henry grinned to himself. This was the ultimate revenge!

"With all due respect," another reporter was saying, "we've seen these publicity stunts before. Bill Veeck and Charlie Finley gave us midgets and disco and green baseballs. Why should we believe Henry isn't just another ploy to sell tickets?"

Henry didn't like the implication. "Hey, I can pitch."

"Prove it," a reporter said, and tossed a baseball to Henry.

"All right." Henry went into a wind-up. But before he could deliver, Mr. Fischer grabbed his arm and stopped him.

"If you want to see him pitch," Mr. Fischer told the reporters, "you can come out to Wrigley."

That night Henry sat on his bed, banging his fist into his old mitt. It was late, but he couldn't sleep. Tomorrow he was supposed to put on a Cubs uniform and join the team. It was hard to imagine himself mixed in with a bunch of men, most of whom were more than twice his age. Every time he tried to picture it, his chest grew tight and he found it difficult to swallow.

There was a knock on his door, and his mother came in. "Can't sleep?" she asked.

Henry nodded. "You think it's going to matter that I've never pitched before?"

"You scared?" Mary asked.

"No, I'm just having a little trouble breathing," Henry replied sarcastically.

"Your father used to say, 'Baseball's a game, and the best players are the ones who love to play the game the most,'" his mother said.

Henry looked up at her. "Did you ever actually see him pitch?"

"Oh, sure," Mary said, taking the mitt from Henry. "I watched every game. They called him the floater. He would mix up floaters and fastballs. 'Always give them what they least expect,' he'd say."

Henry's mom wound up and pitched an imaginary floater.

Henry thought she had pretty good form.

"No one could hit him," Mrs. Rowengartner said wistfully.

Suddenly the door swung open, and Jack burst in with an arm-load of newspapers. "We're famous!" he shouted, tossing one of the papers to Henry. He quickly turned to the sports section. There was a big photo of Henry with his mom and Jack. The headline read: CUBS SIGN CUB.

"Amazing!" Henry gasped.

"That's nothing," Jack said. "The network has canceled its regular programming during the game tomorrow. Forget cable TV, Henry. We're going national!"

"*We're* going national?" Henry's mother repeated. "I'm sorry, Jack, but I don't remember agreeing that you'd be Henry's agent."

"Would you rather have some stranger do it?" Jack asked.

Henry glanced at his mother and shrugged. "Maybe he's right."

"Henry's tired," Mary said, getting up. "I think we'd better let him try to sleep."

"You happy now, Henry?" Jack asked as Mary took his arm and led him out of the room.

"Yeah, thanks, Jack," Henry said. Even though he didn't like the guy, he guessed he had to appreciate what he'd done.

"Tell me this isn't your dream come true," Jack said.

"Let's go, Jack," Mary said, easing him out of Henry's room. "He needs his sleep."

"I'll never get to sleep," Henry said.

"Maybe you could try reading a book," his mother said.

Henry hated reading. He pretended to yawn. "Well, I guess I am pretty tired, after all," he said, lying back on his bed.

Mary smirked and closed the door. Henry lay on his bed and stared wide-eyed at the ceiling, trying to imagine what his first day as a major-league relief pitcher would be like.

# five

*H*enry hardly slept that night. The next morning George and Clark came over and coached him while he practiced throwing at the Little-League field's backstop. Later they all got into Jack's car and drove over to Wrigley Field. They parked in the lot and started walking toward the stadium. Fans going in the gates stopped and pointed at Henry. A few people even yelled his name.

As they got closer to the players' entrance, Henry stopped and turned to his mother. "Uh, Mom, let's say good-bye here."

"But I want to make sure you get in safely," Mary said.

"I appreciate that, Mom," Henry said, "but none of the other Cubs' moms are going to be there."

Mary nodded, but looked disappointed just the same.

"Let him go, Mary," Jack said. "We're due in the owners' box."

Mary bent down and gave Henry a quick kiss on the cheek. "I love you, my little man. We'll meet right here after the game. And don't dawdle."

"Right." Henry waved good-bye and walked toward the players' entrance with his friends.

"I just can't believe this!" George gushed. "Do you realize that in an hour you're going to be on the same field as the Cubs? Playing against the Mets!"

Henry took a deep breath and let it out slowly. It did seem incredible. And totally scary, too. The door to the players' entrance was closed, and he knocked on it. The door opened, and an older man in a security guard's uniform looked out.

"Autographs after the game, boys," he said, and started to close the door.

"Wait," Henry said. "I'm Henry Rowengartner."

"Well, why didn't you say so?" the security guard asked with a smile as he pushed the door open. "Come on in."

Henry turned to George and Clark to say good-bye. Clark handed him a scorecard. "Sign it."

"Why?" Henry asked.

"So we can say we were best friends with you 'when,'" George explained.

"When what?" Henry asked, puzzled.

Clark rolled his eyes. "Just sign it."

Henry scrawled his name on the scorecard. George looked at it and frowned.

"You gotta work on your autograph, Henry," he said. "It's not even in cursive."

Henry went through the players' entrance and down a long hall. He stopped in front of the door marked

LOCKER ROOM. Inside he could hear men talking and laughing. Henry felt his stomach grow tight. He took a deep breath and pushed the door open.

Inside, two dozen men were standing at lockers, changing out of their street clothes and into their baseball uniforms. One of them turned and saw Henry. Then another, and another. Soon the whole locker room was quiet as the players stared at him.

Henry bit his lip and waved meekly. "Uh, hi," he said. "I'm the new pitcher."

The players turned back to their lockers and started talking again as though Henry wasn't there. Almost in a trance, Henry walked down the middle of the locker room. There was Billy Frick, the catcher. Over there was Stan Okie, the golden-glove first baseman. Then Henry saw his hero, Chet Steadman, standing in front of his locker, chewing on a big wad of tobacco. It was just unbelievable. Henry reached into his pocket for a baseball.

"Hey, Rocket," he said cheerfully, "could I have your autograph?"

Steadman looked startled. Then he spit some tobacco juice on the floor. "I don't do autographs," he muttered, and turned away.

Before Henry could feel too disappointed, he heard Martinella shout, "Raffenbooser! Your locker's over here. Suit up!"

Henry went over to his locker. His eyes went wide with delight as he saw his major-league cleats, new uniform, authentic baseball cap, and, best of all, the name ROWENGARTNER written in big black letters on a piece of tape above the locker.

It was a little embarrassing to get undressed with all those big hairy men around him, but the thought of being out on the field got Henry through it. Minutes later, dressed in his new uniform, Henry left the locker room and headed down the runway. Before him lay the most wonderful sight in the world—the broad green field at Wrigley.

Henry stepped out onto the grass. All around him, the Cubs players were taking batting practice, doing stretches and sprints, and throwing balls around to loosen up. Henry felt as though he'd stepped onto hallowed ground. He was taking his place among the gods.

He threw some pitches in the bullpen, and then Martinella called everyone down to the dugout for the start of the game. As Henry walked with the other players toward the dugout, he saw that the stadium was starting to fill up. He heard people calling his name. Looking up, he saw his friends, his mother, and Jack sitting in the owners' box with Mr. Fischer.

"Hi, Henry!" His mother waved.

"Hey, Rowengartner!" George and Clark shouted gleefully. "You stink!"

Jack wasn't even looking at him. He was talking and laughing with Mr. Fischer as if they were old friends.

Henry stepped down into the dugout and held his cap over his heart while they sang the national anthem. The anthem ended and the public-address system crackled on.

"Welcome to Wrigley Field for today's game against

the New York Mets," the announcer said. "Today's attendance is 35,822. That's a sellout, folks!"

The crowd roared, and Henry noticed that several of the Cubs glanced at him and smirked. It was hard to believe, but it seemed the sellout was due to Henry!

"All right, guys, let's do it!" Martinella shouted and slapped his hands. "We're only thirteen games out of first place. Let's win 'em one at a time! The streak starts today! Let's win it!"

None of the players appeared to be listening. Henry was bumped and jostled as he looked for a place to sit on the dugout bench, but he didn't care. Chet Steadman was on the mound, and Henry was going to watch his hero from the most amazing seat in the world—the dugout bench!

The umpire called for the game to begin. On the mound, Steadman threw his last warm-up pitch. Henry was so excited he couldn't stay seated. He jumped up and stood on the dugout steps.

"Gas him, Rocket!" he shouted. "Put some cheese in the kitchen. Big stinky cheddar!"

Steadman straightened up and stared into the dugout with a surprised look on his face. Henry gave him the thumb's-up sign. Steadman looked back at the batter, wound up, and delivered.

*Crack!* The Mets player hammered a single into center field. Steadman glanced dejectedly into the dugout. Henry slouched back into his seat.

The good news was that Steadman settled down and pitched eight strong innings. The bad news was that the Cubs didn't hit. At the end of eight the score was

1–1. Steadman was starting to look tired. In the dugout Martinella got on the phone, and Henry saw a reliever named Leezer get up in the bullpen and start to throw. Out in the crowd, someone yelled, "Where's the kid?" Someone else yelled, "We want Henry!"

Suddenly the whole stadium took up the chant. "We want Henry! We want Henry!"

Embarrassed, Henry slouched down on the dugout bench. On the mound Steadman threw another pitch.

*Crack!* The Mets batter hit a towering shot into left center and stretched it into a triple. In the stands the chant grew louder: *"We want Henry! We want Henry!"*

Down at the end of the dugout, the phone rang. "Oh-oh, it's Fischer," one of the players mumbled.

Martinella picked up the phone. "I'm sorry, Mr. Fischer, but the kid's not ready to pitch yet," he said.

Martinella listened a little longer, then slammed the phone down angrily and turned to Henry. "Warm up. You're going in."

Henry felt a surge of adrenaline rush through him. He was both excited and terrified. As he left the dugout and jogged toward the bullpen, the stadium roared. He got into the bullpen, then turned to watch Steadman pitch.

*Crack!* The Mets batter hit a double, scoring the runner from third. The reliever named Leezer joined Henry at the fence.

"They gotta stick the fork in him," Leezer said. "He's done."

Martinella started out of the dugout toward the pitcher's mound, where Steadman stood with his hands on his hips, shaking his head. The Cubs' manager waved toward the bullpen.

"That's the signal," Leezer said. "You're in."

Henry felt a shiver of fear as he stared out at the huge stadium filled with people. "I'm in?"

The public-address system crackled to life. "And now, pitching for Chicago," the announcer said, "Henry Rowengartner."

The crowd roared.

"Who am I pitching against?" Henry asked nervously.

"Let's see." Leezer rubbed his chin. "Looks like you'll face Alejandro Heddo. A dead fastball hitter."

Henry swallowed. "But that's all I throw."

"Well, good luck," Leezer said with a shrug.

Henry trotted out onto the field. The prospect of pitching was terrifying. The roar of the crowd was deafening. As he jogged, he felt dizzy and unsteady on his feet. Finally he reached the pitcher's mound. Steadman glanced at him for a second, then left the mound with his head down. Martinella dropped the ball into Henry's glove.

"Throw the heat, kid," he said, and turned away.

Henry was alone on the mound. Thirty-five thousand people in the stands were screaming at him. Television cameras were aimed at him. Photographers' cameras clicked like a thousand crickets. His teammates were staring at him and shaking their heads in disbelief. In the visitors' dugout, the Mets were laughing and pointing at him.

And in the on-deck circle, Alejandro Heddo, who

was huge and had incredibly broad shoulders, grinned menacingly, revealing a row of gold teeth.

Henry's stomach churned. He felt faint and light-headed. In a daze of fear and panic, he picked up the rosin bag and bounced it off his hand. A cloud of rosin rose up, and he coughed on it.

Alejandro Heddo stepped up to the plate and ground his cleats into the dirt. Henry was certain he'd never seen a bat that looked so big. Behind the plate, Frick gave him a signal. Henry wasn't sure what it meant, but it didn't matter. He only had one pitch. He got into his stance, rocked back, and fired.

The ball sailed four feet over Heddo's head and smacked into the backstop. Frick threw off his mask and dashed back for it.

"Cover the plate!" he screamed. But Henry was frozen to the pitcher's mound in stunned silence, and the runner from second scored. Henry glanced at the dugout. Martinella had one hand over his eyes and was shaking his head.

Frick threw the ball back to Henry. Heddo took a practice swing, then dug his cleats in again and smiled. With his heart beating wildly, Henry wound up and delivered. The ball smashed into the ground in front of home plate, sending up a shower of dirt, but Frick managed to smother it.

The ball came back to Henry, who was almost dizzy with humiliation and fear. Frick went back into the crouch and gave him a sign. Suddenly Henry stepped off the rubber and started to walk toward the catcher the way he'd seen big-league pitchers do on televi-

sion. Frick frowned and asked the umpire for time-
out, then ran out to see what was wrong.

"What was that signal for?" Henry asked.

"Fastball," the catcher replied. "It's your only pitch."

Henry nodded. "Just checking."

"C'mon now," Frick said. "Put the next one in the
leather."

"You know," Henry said, feeling the sudden urge to
get something off his chest. "I've never actually
pitched before."

"No kidding," Frick smirked.

"Any suggestions?" Henry asked.

"Yeah," said the catcher. "Just throw it nice and
easy."

It didn't sound right to Henry, but Frick was a
catcher with many more years of baseball experience
than he had. So Henry went back to the mound and
threw the next pitch nice and easy.

*Crack!* Heddo took a ferocious swing. Henry
winced, then watched in amazement as the ball
seemed to climb into the stratosphere. A huge groan
swept through the stands. In their dugout, the Mets
were laughing and giving each other high fives. On
the field, Henry's teammates were shaking their heads
sadly. Henry looked up at the owner's box in the
stands. His mother was hiding her face in her hands.
Heddo took a triumphant jog around the diamond.

This is a disaster! Henry thought sadly. I'm totally
messing up! He wished he could run off the field and
hide, but he knew he couldn't. He looked toward the
Cubs dugout for help. Martinella stepped up on the

dugout steps and cupped his hands around his mouth.

"Come on, kid!" he shouted. "Don't lay it in like that. Throw the heat."

The next batter stepped up to the plate. Henry leaned into his windup and heaved. The ball was high and inside. The batter turned his head away and threw himself to the ground as the ball grazed the back of his batting helmet.

There were more groans from the crowd as the umpire gave the batter a base. Henry raised his hand meekly. "Sorry," he said. "My fault."

Now Frick pulled off his catcher's mask and walked toward the mound. Henry stepped off the mound and met him halfway. This was a nightmare.

"They gotta take me out," Henry whispered desperately. "I can't do this."

"That's not my call," the big catcher said, handing the ball back to him. "Just rock and fire."

"What happened to nice and easy?" Henry asked.

"Nice and easy landed in the cheap seats," Frick muttered. "Just throw it."

Now Henry had a man on first. He was supposed to hold him there somehow while getting the next pitch over the plate. As he started his windup, the man on first broke for second. It distracted Henry just enough to throw his aim off. Once again the pitch sailed over Frick and slammed into the backstop.

Frick scrambled back for the ball. The Mets player rounded second and tried to go for third. Frick rocketed the ball to the third baseman, who tagged the runner out.

The inning was over. It was a miracle, but instead of

feeling relieved, Henry was miserable. He'd thrown five pitches, and each one had been worse than the previous. He slunk back to the dugout. Martinella and the other players ignored him, which was just as well. Henry paused to watch as the first Cubs batter stepped up to the plate. When he was sure that the other Cubs were watching the batter, he slipped out of the dugout and headed for the locker room.

There were tears in his eyes. His major-league debut had been a disaster.

Instead of going home, Henry went out to Fox Lake, to the duck blind. The boat was there, and he could see that Clark and George had been working on it. It appeared that at least they would accomplish something good that summer. Meanwhile, Henry had had the chance of a lifetime and he'd blown it.

Henry shook his head sadly. He'd totally humiliated himself. He knew that somewhere out there Rick Sherman was laughing. He knew that Clark and George were feeling bad for him. He knew his mother would tell him that he still needed time to adjust to the big leagues and the pressure. But Henry had to decide whether he could go through this torture again. It was one thing to have a hundred-mile-an-hour fast-ball. But if he didn't have control, it was useless.

Henry looked down and picked up a rock. A large round buoy floated in the lake about sixty feet away. Henry made up his mind. If he could hit the buoy, he'd go back to the Cubs. If he missed, he was finished with the big leagues.

He wound up and hurled.

*Splash!* The rock hit the water two feet to the left of the buoy. Henry sighed. Maybe he'd try two out of three. He picked up another stone and held it under his chin with both hands. Then he reared back and hurled.

*Clang!* The rock ricocheted off the buoy. Henry smiled, picked up another rock, and threw it.

*Clang!* Henry's smile grew into a wide grin. He was still in the majors!

**H**enry spent the summer with his arm in a cast. It wasn't fun. He couldn't play ball.

**T**hey tied a heavy sofa cushion to Clark's chest and put a football helmet on his head for protection. George stood behind him, wearing a cushion and a colander on his head. Clark squatted down like a catcher.

**F**ischer pulled Jack to the side and whispered urgently to him. Henry thought he heard Mr. Fischer ask Jack if Mary was going to be a problem.

Jack burst in with an arm-load of newspapers. "We're famous!" he shouted.

**"T**ry dealing from your have-to," Chet Steadman said. "The stuff you use when you feel like quitting."

**H**enry got into his batting stance. "Sorry, son," said the umpire, "but you're going to have to get into the batter's box."

**T**hey were the most incredible ten days of Henry's life. The Cubs kept winning, and he kept earning saves. Every moment he wasn't on the field, it seemed as if he was being interviewed by a different newspaper, magazine, or television show.

**T**he next spring Henry played right field for the Oak Park Pirates again. The team was pretty much the same except Mrs. Rowengartner was now the coach, and Chet was the assistant coach.

# six

The next day at practice, Martinella was waiting on the field for Henry.

"Okay, kid," the manager said, "you're fined five hundred dollars for leaving the game early yesterday."

"Five hundred dollars!" Henry gasped. "That's, like, six years' allowance!"

But Martinella wasn't listening. He'd turned and was waving at Chet Steadman. "Get over here, Steadman!"

Henry watched his hero saunter slowly toward them. Martinella took a ball out and tossed it to Steadman. "You're working with the kid."

Steadman looked disgusted. "I ain't playing wet nurse to a twelve-year-old."

"You ain't playing much of anything these days," Martinella reminded him.

Steadman glared at him, then turned to Henry. "Okay, kid, let's go to the bullpen."

For the next hour, Henry was in a daze of happiness. Chet Steadman was giving him tips and advice on how to pitch! And even though Steadman acted as though he hated doing it, Henry noticed that he watched every pitch and always knew what adjustments Henry had to make to keep the ball in the strike zone.

Then the game began. The Cubs played well. By the bottom of the eighth inning, they were ahead 6–5 with one man out and a man on first. Martinella was a bundle of excited energy.

"Okay!" he shouted. "Rogers, you're on deck. Pinch-hit for Leezer! Smith and Bauvier, get out to the bullpen and warm up."

Henry was relieved that he hadn't been sent to the bullpen. He knew he still needed a lot of work before he was ready to throw in the major leagues, and he was content to spend the game sitting in the dugout, spitting sunflower-seed husks.

Near him, Steadman stood up and ambled down to Martinella. "Let the kid pitch," Steadman said. Henry nearly choked on a sunflower seed.

"The kid?" Martinella frowned. "You just started working with him. You really think he's ready?"

"No, but he's the hardest damn thrower on this team, so what do you have to lose?" Steadman asked.

"What're you now, the pitching coach?" Martinella asked.

"Maybe I should be," Steadman replied.

Martinella rubbed his chin and thought about it, then turned toward Henry. "Reeminferter! Warm up. You're going in."

Henry barely had time to warm up before the Cubs hit into a double play and had to take the field again. As he walked unhappily toward the mound, he couldn't help thinking that there were nine other pitchers on the team. Why did Martinella have to choose him?

Henry glanced up in the stands at the owners' box. His mother and his friends were watching with Jack, Mr. Fischer, and some business executives who were interested in endorsements. The night before, Jack had said the business executives would be coming to make sure that Henry was "the real thing" before they invested a lot of money in him.

As Henry stepped onto the pitcher's mound, he felt like a fake. He knew he wasn't ready. It wasn't fair that they were making him pitch again. It was the top of the ninth, and there were only three outs left. Couldn't someone else get them?

Once again, Henry's heart started to pound, and his mouth grew dry. Frick gave him the sign, and Henry delivered the first pitch. The ball was low and inside and nicked the batter on the toe. The next thing Henry knew, the batter was given first base.

Henry rolled his eyes. *Here we go again.* Frick threw the ball back and motioned Henry to calm down. Henry glanced to the dugout and saw Chet Steadman get up and walk toward him. Steadman walked out to the edge of the pitcher's mound. He stuck his hands in his back pockets and spit some tobacco juice on the ground.

"What are you doing out here?" he asked.

"I'm pitching," Henry replied.

"No, you're quitting," Steadman said.

That hurt. "What am I supposed to do?" Henry asked.

"Try dealing from your *have-to*," Steadman said.

"My what?" Henry asked, confused.

"Your have-to. The stuff you use when you feel like quitting."

"Are you speaking English?" Henry asked.

"Look, everybody's half win and half lose," Steadman said. "The lose half is afraid."

"Right." Henry nodded. That much he understood.

"The win half is fearless."

"I'm with you," Henry said, although he hadn't been in touch with that half recently.

"The have-to gets rid of the afraid," Steadman said.

"But where is the have-to?" Henry asked.

"Inside, with the fearless."

Henry still didn't know what Steadman was talking about. "Uh, could you start over?"

Steadman squinted impatiently at him. "You got the have-to, don't you?"

Henry quickly nodded.

"Play ball!" the umpire shouted.

"Okay, kid," Steadman said. "Let's see it." He turned and left the mound. Henry looked down at the baseball in his hand and wondered what the heck Steadman had been talking about. The next batter stepped into the batter's box. Henry took a deep breath and felt his heart start to pound again. Suddenly he heard cheering from his left. Looking over, he saw Clark, George, and his mother in the seats right behind the dugout. They must've snuck down to be closer to him. Henry smiled. He went into the windup and threw.

*Crack!* The batter made contact. Oh, no! Henry groaned and turned, expecting to see the ball sail out of the stadium. But he couldn't find the ball. Instead he heard two soft pops—each like the sound a ball made when it smacked into a glove.

The crowd roared. Henry looked around, bewildered.

"Way to pitch, Henry!" Stan Okie said, tossing him the ball. Henry realized two players from the opposing team were leaving the field. That could only mean one thing—he'd thrown a double-play ball!

Suddenly the infielders were talking to him.

"One more out, kid!" shouted Mannie Suárez, the shortstop.

"Just get this last one!" yelled Tony Fern, the second baseman.

Once again Henry heard the cameras clicking. The fans were screaming. For the first time he started to feel good. Just one more out, he told himself. *Just one more!*

Henry wound up and delivered. Even before the ball left his hand he knew it felt right. At the plate the batter didn't even swing.

"Strike one!" The umpire shouted. The crowd cheered and Frick had a big grin on his face. The batter shook his head and dug his cleats into the batter's box.

Henry threw again. The batter swung! Henry winced, but heard nothing.

"Strike two!" The umpire shouted.

All of a sudden the stadium was on its feet, roaring. Suárez, Fern, and Okie were shouting at him. Clark, George, and Mary were crossing every finger they had. Henry squeezed the ball in his pitching hand and stood perfectly still. The crowd began to quiet down. The batter choked up, ready to swing.

Henry wound up and hurled.

"Strike three!"

Henry felt a huge weight rise off his shoulders. He was faint with relief. Finally, he'd done something right! As players rushed toward him from the dugout and field, Henry raised his arms in triumph. He'd just recorded his first major-league save!

The celebration swept Henry back into the locker room. Everyone came over and shook his hand or patted him on the head and told him he'd thrown some great pitches. Even Martinella came over and said he'd never doubted Henry's abilities for a minute.

After a while the celebration died down, and the other players headed for the showers. But Henry was still incredibly pumped. As he took off his Cubs cap and put it on the shelf of his locker, he noticed a baseball lying there. Henry picked it up and saw that it was signed "Rocket." He looked up and saw Chet Steadman in front of his own locker, smiling at him.

It was too good to be true. Henry looked back at his locker and realized he didn't want to change into his street clothes and leave the stadium yet. He wanted to go back out and relive the moment of his first triumph.

Seconds later he walked back out onto the field. The stadium was empty, or so he thought. Suddenly he heard a familiar voice shout, "Hey, Rowengartner!"

Henry looked up and saw Clark and George in the stands. Together they shouted, "You stink!"

Henry grinned and waved for them to come down to the field. Soon they were playing phantom baseball. George played first base, Henry pitched, and Clark batted. Henry threw an invisible ball and Clark swung an invisible bat.

"It's a dribbler!" Henry shouted, racing after the imaginary ball while Clark ran toward first. "Rowengartner has no time to throw to first! He's going to have to tag Krieger!"

But Clark beat him to first base. "Safe!" he shouted.

The boys stood around first base, catching their breaths. Before Henry walked back to the mound, he snuck George the baseball Steadman had signed. Henry stepped onto the mound. Clark took a lead off first.

George quickly tagged him. "You're out!" he shouted. "Unbelievable! The hidden-ball play!"

Suddenly the boys heard laughter from the dugout. A bunch of Cubs in street clothes had come out to watch. Henry gave them an embarrassed grin. Then he noticed that his mother and Chet Steadman were standing next to each other, talking. He couldn't hear what they were saying, but Mary smiled and seemed a little breathless. Steadman looked down shyly and scuffed his shoe against the dugout steps. Henry looked around, but Jack was nowhere in sight.

# seven

It was time for the West Coast swing. Henry's mother and his friends came along for the ride to the airport. The crowd of fans and reporters was so thick that a couple of the Cubs' security men had to escort Henry to the gate where the charter jet would leave. Martinella came over and put his hand on Henry's shoulder.

"Don't worry, Mrs. Reevenblubber, we'll take good care of your son," the Cubs' manager said.

"Now, you do everything Mr. Martinella says," Mary said, wiping a tear out of her eye. "Be a good boy. I'll see you in ten days. You'll be home just in time for the start of school."

Henry turned to his friends.

"Eat your vegetables," Clark said.

"Get plenty of rest," George said.

"Stay cool, guys," Henry said, giving them high fives.

"Final boarding," a gate attendant said.

Henry turned to go in. Suddenly he heard his mother call, "Henry!"

He turned around and saw her toss a tube of sun block in a high arc toward him. Henry got under it and made the grab. He waved at Mary one last time and got on the plane.

A little while later Henry found himself sitting next to Chet Steadman.

"Thanks for signing the baseball," Henry said.

"No problem," Chet said. "But do me a favor and don't call me Rocket. Nobody calls me that anymore."

There was a question Henry was dying to ask. "Please don't take this the wrong way. But I was wondering how come you're throwing so slow these days."

"I don't know what my arm will do if I heat it up again," Chet replied.

"Hey!" Henry said, getting an idea. "Maybe you should go see the doctor who fixed my arm!"

Chet laughed. It seemed to Henry that maybe they could be friends.

The team arrived in Los Angeles just in time to get on the bus and go out to Dodger Stadium for an evening game.

The game was close. In the seventh inning, with the Dodgers ahead 3–2, Martinella sent Henry in to pitch. Henry started off feeling nervous, but managed to retire the side with two strikeouts and a pop-up. As he returned to the dugout, Martinella grabbed him.

"You good for another inning?" the manager asked.

"You bet," Henry said.

"Good. You're on deck."

Henry stared at him in disbelief. "I'm what?"

"You're batting after Fern," Martinella said.

Henry felt his stomach begin to churn. Chet overheard the conversation and quickly came over.

"Sal," he said, "you can't let Henry bat. He'll get killed out there."

"Hey, he's gonna have to learn sometime," Martinella snapped, and walked away.

Chet turned to Henry, shrugged, and went to the dugout. "Better do what he says."

Henry walked slowly out to the on-deck circle. He picked up a bat, swung it, and almost lost his balance.

"Choke up," Chet yelled from the dugout.

Henry's mouth felt dry, and his palms were sweating. The idea of facing a major-league pitcher was frightening. He glanced back at Chet. "You know, there's a lot to be said for designated hitters."

"Stay low," Chet said.

At the plate, Fern went down swinging. As Henry walked toward the batter's box, the Cubs started yelling encouragement.

"Powder it, Henry!"

"Show him where you live!"

"Let the big dog eat!"

Henry got into his batting stance. On the mound, the Dodgers' pitcher frowned.

"Sorry, son," said the umpire, "but you're going to have to get into the batter's box."

Henry took three giant steps and stood at the very back corner of the batter's box. The Dodgers' pitcher went into a crouch and glared at him.

*Ohmigodohmigodohmigodohmigod!* Henry cowered in the corner of the box as the pitcher wound up and delivered a sizzling curveball straight at Henry's head!

Henry hit the dirt with his eyes closed as the ball broke back outside.

"Ball one!" the umpire shouted.

Henry scowled, stood up, and dusted himself off. The Dodgers' pitcher delivered again, and again Henry dove out of the way.

"Ball two!" the umpire shouted.

The Dodgers' pitcher threw his mitt down on the mound. "That kid's got no strike zone!" he shouted.

"Just pitch!" the umpire shouted back.

Henry stood up and dusted himself off again. The pitcher threw two more balls. Henry couldn't believe it.

"Take your base," the umpire said.

"Excellent!" Henry tossed the bat aside and jogged down to first base. The Cubs cheered. Mannie Suárez stepped into the batter's box. Henry tried to take a small lead off first base. The Dodgers' pitcher wheeled and threw to the first baseman.

For a split second, Henry froze.

"Get back!" the Cubs shouted from the dugout.

Henry dove back to the bag, just beating the throw. The first baseman tossed the ball back to the pitcher. Emboldened, Henry took a lead off first again.

"We want a pitcher, not an underwear snitcher!" Henry shouted.

In the dugout, the Cubs laughed. The Dodgers' pitcher glowered at him, then wheeled and threw to first again.

This time the throw went over the first baseman's head!

"Go, Henry, go!" the Cubs shouted. Henry took off for second and dove in headfirst, just ahead of the tag.

"Safe!" shouted the second-base umpire.

The Dodgers' pitcher glared at Henry, who stuck out his tongue. The next pitch got away and hit Suárez on the back. Suddenly there was one out and two men on. Stan Okie stepped up to the plate.

*Crack!* Okie creamed the next pitch into the gap between center and right. As Henry took off for third he saw the ball roll to the wall. He knew it was deep enough to let Suárez score the winning run from first.

As Henry rounded third he heard footsteps at his heels.

"Hurry! Can't you run any faster?" It was Suárez, right behind him.

"This is as fast as I can go!" Henry gasped. Out of the corner of his eye he saw the center fielder throw the ball to the cutoff man, who spun and hurled the ball home.

"Slide!" Suárez shouted. Henry slid. Suárez slid. A cloud of dust kicked up around home plate.

"Safe! Safe!" the umpire shouted.

The Cubs won that game.

It was late when the team got back to the hotel. Henry and Chet walked down a long corridor and stopped outside Henry's room. Henry had never stayed in a hotel alone before.

"Uh, it's really cool how everybody gets their own rooms," he said, trying to hide his nervousness.

"In the old days we used to have roommates," Chet said.

"Who'd you room with?" Henry asked.

"Oh, a lot of people. None of them are around anymore."

"Well, good night, Chet," Henry said.

"Good night, Henry," Chet said.

Henry stepped into his room and closed the door behind him. The lights were on, and he saw that there were two beds in the room. One of the beds had been turned down, but the room still felt very empty. He was nearly two thousand miles away from home, and all alone in a big hotel. He opened his bag and put on his pajamas, then went into the bathroom and washed up.

He came back out, got into bed, and turned off the lights.

Even though he was tired, he lay awake for a long time.

Finally he got out of bed and went out into the hall. He went down to Chet's room and knocked. Chet opened the door and smiled down at him.

"Your bed uncomfortable?" he asked.

Henry nodded.

"You might want to try that one," Chet said, pointing to the spare bed in his room. "I think you'll like it better."

Henry got into the bed. In no time he was asleep.

# eight

*T*hey were the most incredible ten days of Henry's life. The Cubs kept winning, and he kept earning saves. Every moment he wasn't on the field, it seemed as if he was being interviewed by a different newspaper, magazine, or television show. He even made the cover of *Sports Illustrated*! The best thing about it was having Chet around to help show him the ropes.

Finally it was time to fly home. The plane landed at O'Hare late at night, but as Chet and Henry came out of the jetway, they saw that the gate area was wall-to-wall fans and reporters.

"Chet!" a reporter shouted. "You're one game out of first place with ten to play. How's it going to turn out?"

"Hey, we're the Cubs," Chet replied. "You never know."

"How does it feel to be outpitched by a twelve-year-old?" another reporter asked.

Henry was afraid Chet would get angry, but the older pitcher just smiled. "I don't care whose coattails we ride, as long as we get that championship ring."

Henry and Chet had to stop. The crowd of fans and media was blocking their path.

"Henry!" Mary shouted. Henry saw her at the back of the crowd and waved, but there was no way he could reach her. Suddenly Chet picked him up. "Give him some room, folks. Back off!"

Chet started pushing through the crowd toward Mary. Finally he reached her.

"Let's go!" he gasped. The next thing Henry knew, he, his mom, and Chet were jogging through the airport, pursued by reporters and autograph hounds.

They reached the sidewalk and dove into a waiting limousine.

"Go!" Chet shouted at the driver, and the limo pulled out into traffic. Inside, Henry and his mother settled into the back seat.

"Thanks for getting Henry out of that," Mary said.

"No problem," Chet replied. "You can drop me off at the next terminal. I'll get a cab."

"No way," Henry said. "We'll give you a ride."

"Henry's right," Mary said. "We have this whole huge limousine that Mr. Fischer gave us. Drop us off, and I'm sure the driver will take you home." She turned to the chauffeur. "Would that be okay?"

"Sure." The chauffeur nodded.

Chet smiled at Mary. "Thanks."

For the next few minutes they sat silently in the back of the limo. Henry was glad that jerk Jack wasn't around. He liked Chet a lot more. Then he had an idea.

"Hey, it's cocktail time," he said, leaning toward the limo's bar. "You want the usual, Chet?"

"Please," Chet said with a smile.

Henry poured a Perrier® into a glass with ice and squeezed in a small slice of lime, then handed it to Chet.

"Where did you learn that?" his mother asked.

"On the road, babe," Henry replied, jokingly. "What'll you have?"

"Club soda . . . babe," his mother replied.

Henry glanced down at the bar. "No club soda. I have French water, Swiss water . . . *Avec gaz. Sans gaz.*"

"French, please," Mary said. "And no gas."

Henry made her the same drink he'd made Chet. Then he turned down the lights in the back of the limo and found a radio station with romantic piano music.

"Henry . . ." His mother started to say.

"What?" Henry asked innocently. "I happen to like this music." He started to snap his fingers to the music. Mary and Chet laughed nervously. Then Chet held up his glass.

"Here's to a terrific kid and a great pitcher," he said.

"I'll drink to that," said Mary, clinking her glass against his. Henry wasn't certain, but he got the feeling they liked each other.

The lights were on when they got home. Mary asked Chet if he'd like to come in for some coffee, and the chauffeur said he'd be glad to wait. Henry was totally surprised when he pulled open the door. Inside, the living room was filled with BMX bikes, boxes of Reebok® sneakers, cases of Pepsi®, and cartons of Wheaties®. George and Clark were each perched on a bike, wearing new sneakers and warmups.

"Hey, feeling good! Looking good!" George said with a grin. He and Clark gave Henry high fives.

"Where'd you get all this stuff?" Henry asked, amazed.

Jack came in from the kitchen, wearing a brandnew jogging outfit. "It's all yours, Henry. Welcome home."

"This is all mine?" Henry couldn't believe it.

"Yup," Jack said with a big smile. "It's all perks. Because thanks to me, you are now a spokesperson for Reebok®, BMX, Pepsi®, and Wheaties®."

"Are we going to be the coolest guys in school or what?" Clark asked.

Chet and Mary entered the room. "Uh, Jack," Mary said, "this is —"

"I know," Jack said, shaking Chet's hand. "The Rocket. More like the firecracker these days. How's the gimpy wing?"

"Good, thanks," Chet said, setting his jaw.

Sensing a tense situation, Henry turned to his friends. "Uh, why don't you guys go upstairs?"

Mary said she'd go into the kitchen and make some coffee. Henry pretended to follow her, but he stayed near the doorway and listened to Chet and Jack.

"Henry's told me a lot about you," Chet was saying.

"You've really got the endorsement machine in gear."

"That's what agents are for," Jack said proudly.

"Don't you think Henry's got enough to worry about, just pitching in the majors?" Chet asked.

"Don't you think you should mind your own business?" Jack replied in a distinctly unfriendly tone.

Mary called Henry into the kitchen to help her get the tray for the coffee. When they went back out to the living room, Chet was gone.

The next day Henry and his friends rode their new bikes to school. As soon as the other kids saw him, Henry was mobbed by autograph seekers. Rick Sherman, Greg Teaser, and some of the other Pirates stood nearby, watching in jealous disbelief. Soon the mob had separated Henry from Clark and George.

"Hey, aren't you coming inside?" George yelled.

"As soon as I can," Henry shouted back, still signing autographs. George and Clark glanced at each other, annoyed.

"We'll catch you later," Clark muttered. Then he and George went into school.

Henry didn't see his friends again until later in the morning. He was at his locker, packing some books in his book bag.

"What are you doing?" Clark asked.

"I have to go," Henry said.

"You get to leave now?" George asked, surprised. "It's not even lunch."

"I got a game," Henry explained. "The Cubs are going for first place today. It's super important. You guys coming?"

George and Clark glanced at each other. "We can't come to every game, Henry. We have to stay in school."

"We'll see you after," Clark said.

Henry bit his lip. "I can't, guys. Reebok®'s throwing a big party. I have to go."

George looked down at the floor, and Clark stared down the hall. Suddenly no one knew what to say.

"Well, uh, I guess I'll see you tomorrow," Henry said. George and Clark sort of nodded and walked away. Henry knew he should have felt superexcited by what was happening, but all he felt was weird.

It was the bottom of the ninth and two men were out. The bases were loaded and the Cubs were behind by one run. If they could somehow win, they'd be in first place. In the dugout, Martinella looked down at the batting order and shook his head.

"Darn," he muttered. "It's the bottom of the order."

"Pinch-hit the kid," Chet said. "We'll get a walk out of it and tie the game."

"That's the stupidest idea I ever heard!" Martinella said with a frown. Then he blinked. "Henry, get out there. And don't swing at anything. I just want a walk!"

Henry jumped up and jogged out to the on-deck circle. This time he decided to loosen up each arm separately, like the big hitters did. First he swung the bat with his left arm. But when he swung it with his right arm, the bat tomahawked over his head as if he were chopping wood. The bat almost flew out of his hand.

"Whoa!" Henry gasped "What a cut!"

"Batter up!" the umpire shouted.

Henry stepped up to the plate. The pitcher reared back and hurled a sizzler right past Henry's midsection.

"Strike one!" the umpire shouted.

*Strike?* Henry couldn't believe it. He stared into the dugout.

"Stay low!" Martinella shouted. Henry crouched down. The pitcher threw again.

"Strike two!" the umpire shouted.

Henry's jaw dropped. They'd found his strike zone! On the mound, the pitcher grinned as if he knew he had Henry's number. In the dugout, Martinella shook his head in disgust. Chet cupped his hands around his mouth and shouted. "Protect the plate!"

The next thing Henry knew, the Cubs were shouting at him to hit. Henry knew he had nothing to lose, because the pitcher was sure to strike him out if he didn't swing. Henry ground his feet into the dirt and pulled the bat back. He glared over his left shoulder at the pitcher.

The pitcher reared back and delivered a high fastball, obviously hoping Henry would go out of the strike zone for it. Henry did, tomahawking the bat over his head.

*Crack!* The bat made contact! The ball shot in a straight line right out of the stadium. Henry had hit a grand slam! The whole stadium went berserk! The Cubs were in first place!

# nine

The next day before lunch, Henry was at his locker when he felt someone tap him on his shoulder. He turned to find Clark and George behind him. George was carrying the prop for their boat.

"Can I have your autograph?" Clark asked.

"I already gave you my autograph," Henry said.

"Yeah, but that was after you became the youngest person ever to sign with the Cubs," George explained. "Now he wants your autograph because you're the first twelve-year-old pitcher in major-league history to hit a pinch grand slam."

Henry gave Clark the autograph, and the three boys walked into the cafeteria. Becky Fraker immediately waved at them from the table where she was sitting with Tiffany James and some other popular girls.

"Hi, Henry!" Becky called.

"Forget it," Clark said nervously. "I'm not sitting over there."

"Don't worry," Henry said with newfound confidence. "We'll be fine. They're just kids."

George stared at him with a puzzled look. "So are we, Henry."

Henry blinked. For a moment there, it actually felt as if he'd forgotten. He and his friends went over and sat down at the table. George put the prop down beside him.

"What's that?" Becky asked.

"It's the prop for the boat we're working on," Henry explained.

"You have a boat?" Becky asked.

"Kind of," Henry said.

"We have a boat," Becky said. "But I always have to ride in it with my parents."

Clark nudged Henry and whispered, "Tell her you'll take her for a ride."

Henry was too nervous and shook his head. Clark nudged him again. "Go ahead, tell her."

Henry took a deep breath and tried to summon up his courage. Just then the bell rang and it was time to head to the next class.

"See you later, Henry," Becky said with a smile, then grabbed her books and left. Henry shook his head, disappointed now that he'd missed the opportunity to talk to her.

"Man, you were close," Clark said as they left the cafeteria.

"When we finish the boat I'll ask her," Henry said.

"As soon as we get this prop on, we'll almost be there," George said. "Let's go right after school."

"I can't," Henry said. "Jack set up a photo shoot for Pepsi®. I'll meet you after that."

Both of his friends stared at him.

"You've said that before," George muttered.

"This'll only take an hour," Henry promised. "I swear."

"Sure." Clark nodded dubiously and pulled at George's sleeve. "Come on, dude, we better get to class."

The shoot for Pepsi® took a lot longer than Henry expected. The sun was starting to go down by the time he got out to Fox Lake. George and Clark were busy working on the boat. Their hands and clothes were covered with dirt and grease.

"Look who decided to show up," George muttered.

"They kept me there for hours," Henry tried to explain. "You think I like doing that stuff?"

"I don't know," George said sharply. "Do you?"

Henry could see that his friends were upset. "Look, I'm sorry. Let's just work on the boat."

"Sounds good," Clark said. But George shook his head.

"I'm not working on the boat just because you say to," he said angrily.

"So I'm supposed to work on it alone?" Henry asked.

"Great idea!" George said bitterly. "Work on it alone." George started to walk away, but Henry grabbed his arm. He knew why they were angry.

"You guys thought this baseball thing was a great idea," he said.

"Don't lay it off on us!" George snapped, slapping Henry's hand away. Henry grabbed him again, and he and George fell to the ground, wrestling. Clark tried to pull them apart.

"Break it up, you guys," he shouted. "You're supposed to be friends."

Clark managed to separate Henry and George, but George stormed away angry. Henry went home feeling bad. His mother and Jack were discussing business in the living room.

"If you could just sign this," Jack said, handing a piece of paper to Mary.

"What is it?" Henry's mother asked.

"Just insurance," Jack said, and turned to Henry. "How'd the Pepsi® shoot go?"

"Great," Henry said as sarcastically as he could. But Jack didn't pick up on it. All he cared about was money.

The next day after practice Chet gave Henry a ride home. They rode in Chet's truck. Usually Chet played country music and talked a lot, but today he was quiet.

"Hey," Henry said as they neared his house, "what's eating you?"

"Nothing," Chet said.

"C'mon," Henry said. "We could win the division tomorrow. Maybe we'll win the pennant for the first time since 1945. After that we'd have a shot at the World Series. Isn't that what you always wanted?"

Chet glanced at him and sighed. "You're a great kid, Henry, but don't take this game too seriously because someday it'll be over. Your gift will be gone and you'll have to rely on who you are. You got a great mom. You got great friends. That's your real life. And that's what's going to see you through."

Henry didn't know what had brought this on, but he knew Chet well enough to take what he said seriously. Chet dropped him off at the house, and Henry went inside. Jack was in the kitchen, on the phone. When Henry came in, he hung up.

"Hey!" Jack said crossly. "I had a limo waiting for you outside the stadium to take you to a photo shoot. Where were you?"

"Chet gave me a ride home," Henry said.

"Well, you better get ready," Jack said. "You've got to be there in fifteen minutes."

Henry thought about what Chet had said in the car. He thought about the fight he'd had with George, and how he hated not having time to hang out with his friends. "I'm not going," he said.

"Excuse me?" Jack pretended he hadn't heard correctly.

"I'm going to play with my friends," Henry said, and turned for the stairs. Suddenly Jack grabbed his arm and spun him around.

"You can't just blow off a photo shoot," he said.

"Get out of my face, Jack," Henry said, pulling his arm away. But Jack grabbed him again.

"Don't walk away when I'm talking to you," Jack shouted. "Show some respect!"

"You're not my father!" Henry shouted back.

"That's right," Jack yelled. "I'm not your father. In fact, I'm not sure your mother even knows who your father is! Your father's some guy who left town."

"That's enough!" Henry and Jack turned and saw Mary standing on the stairs, a shocked look on her face. "How could you say that about Henry's father?"

"Hey, it's common knowledge," Jack replied with a smirk. Mary glared at him.

"Get out," she said, just barely able to control her anger.

"Mary—" Jack started to apologize.

"I never want to see you again," Mary said, pointing at the door. But Jack just laughed.

"You're going to be seeing a lot of me," he said as he headed toward the door. "We're moving to New York."

"What?" Mary looked puzzled.

"Henry's been sold to the Yankees," Jack said, pulling some papers out of his pocket. Henry recognized them as the "insurance" papers Jack had had Mary sign the previous night. "You signed a contract authorizing the trade."

Mary's eyes widened. "Why, you snake."

"The Cubs wouldn't trade me," Henry said. "They said I was their best pitcher."

"Time to grow up, kid," Jack replied smugly. "This game isn't about baseball; it's about money."

Mary walked across the living room. She ripped the gold chain off her neck, balled it in her hand, and slapped Jack in the face. He fell backward through the doorway. Mary grabbed the door and slammed it shut.

"All right!" Henry gave her a high five. But his mother looked sad.

"Settle down," she said softly. "Sit. I want to tell you about your father."

Henry sat down. Mary sat next to him and clasped her hands. "Henry," she began, "I got married when I was a teenager . . . "

Henry couldn't stand seeing her go through this pain. "I know about Dad. He left you when you were pregnant with me."

Mary stared at him with wide eyes. "How did you know?"

"Grandma told me when I was in second grade," Henry said.

"Why didn't you tell me?" Tears formed in her eyes.

"I don't know," Henry said with shrug. "I guess I thought you liked telling me about him being lost at sea, and how he was a great pitcher. I didn't want to hurt your feelings."

Mary wiped the tears out of her eyes and smiled. "I just wanted you to have someone you could look up to."

"I do, Mom," Henry said, putting his hand on hers. "I've got you."

His mother smiled at him.

"There's just one thing," Henry added. "You were kind of pushing it with that story about Dad throwing the floater. No one strikes out anybody with a floater."

His mother just hugged him and didn't reply.

# ten

The next day Henry went down to Fox Lake. George and Clark were putting the finishing touches on the boat.

"Hey, guys," Henry said. "You're launching today, huh?"

His friends ignored him and kept working.

"Okay," Clark told George. "It's ready."

Henry watched as Clark and George got into the boat. George stepped to the back and reached for the starter rope. Henry shoved his hands in his pockets and felt bad. It looked as if his friends were going to leave without him. Then George looked up, and his eyes met Henry's. The two friends just stared at each other for a moment.

"Okay," George said begrudgingly. "Get in."

Henry grinned and jumped into the boat. George pulled the rope, and the engine coughed to life. The next thing Henry knew, they were headed toward the Lake Club.

They picked up Becky, Edith, and Tiffany, and had a great afternoon with the boat. By the time Henry got back home, he'd made up his mind about something.

The next day was the season finale against the Mets. If the Cubs won, they'd win their division. It would give them a shot at the league championship, which they hadn't won since 1945. Before the game, Henry went to the front office and told Mr. Fischer he wouldn't be playing for the Cubs *or* the Yankees next year.

Mr. Fischer nearly fainted, but there was nothing he could do. Henry insisted that today was his final game. Then he went down to the locker room and got into his uniform.

Martinella came in and announced that Chet Steadman would be the starting pitcher.

"Aren't you gonna go with the kid?" Chet asked, surprised.

"The kid'll be there for me," Martinella replied. "But in a big game like this, I'll go with experience. Even if it is you."

Henry noticed that Chet bit his lip and rubbed his hands together nervously.

"You all right?" Henry asked.

"Look at me," Chet said with a nervous grin. "I'm shaking. I feel like a rookie again."

"Just go with your *have-to*," Henry said.

"My what?" Chet asked, puzzled.

"Just win it, Rocket," Henry said, patting him on the shoulder.

They went out to the dugout. Martinella was trying to get the team revved up.

"Okay, this is the big one," he told them. "We win this and we're in the play-offs. Steadman's on the mound. Back him up. Play hard. Let's go!"

At the end of six innings, the Cubs were ahead 2–1. Chet was pitching his best game in years. But as he started to throw in the top of the seventh, Henry saw that something was wrong. Each time Chet threw the ball, he winced in pain. His pitches were starting to lose some of their sting and accuracy. Before long, the bases were loaded. Chet made one last heroic play, tagging a runner out at home, and saving the inning. Then he trudged toward the dugout. All the Cubs jumped up and patted him on the back, congratulating him. Instead of sitting, Chet walked straight up to Martinella.

"Stick a fork in me, Sal," he said. "I'm done."

"You gave me seven great innings," Martinella said, patting him on the shoulder. "Save the rest for the play-offs."

But Chet shook his head. "No, I mean, I'm done. I felt my arm go out there. It's gone for good."

Martinella nodded gravely. "Well, you'll make a good manager. Just let me finish the season before you take my job, okay?"

Chet smiled and sat down next to Henry.

"Rowengartner!" Martinella shouted.

Henry sat up straight. "What'd you say?" He

couldn't believe the manager had actually pronounced his name correctly.

"You're going in," Martinella said.

Henry turned to Chet. "Your last game and my last game all in one day."

"What?" Chet didn't understand.

"Didn't you hear?" Henry asked. "I'm playing for the Pirates next year."

"You're going to Pittsburgh?" Chet asked, astonished.

Henry shook his head. "Oak Park."

In the eighth inning Henry struck out two Mets and got the third out on a foul fly. The Cubs didn't score in the bottom of the eighth, and they went into the top of the ninth still ahead 2–1. As Henry started to leave the dugout for the mound, Martinella stopped him.

"Please," the Cubs' manager said. "Get us through this inning and I'll never ask you for anything else as long as I live."

Henry smiled. "Okay, but this is the last time."

Not looking where he was going, Henry stepped right onto a loose baseball. Suddenly he flipped into the air and landed hard on his right side. A loud gasp rose from the crowd. Henry stood up and brushed himself off. He looked up into the owners' box and saw that his mother and friends looked worried. He waved to them as if to say he was all right.

Henry got to the mound and threw a warm-up pitch. As the ball left his hand, he realized something was wrong. The ball seemed to go in slow motion. Frick threw it back and Henry hurled the next warm-up pitch as hard as he could. The ball practically limped through the air! Suddenly Henry realized what had happened. He'd lost his magic arm when he fell on his side a moment ago. All he had now was a typical twelve-year-old's pitch!

A big Met stepped into the batter's box. Henry started to sweat. If he threw that slow pitch, the guy would cream it! Frick signaled for a fastball. Henry shook his head. He did the same when the catcher signaled for a curve, screwball, and a slider. Finally the catcher stood up in frustration. Suddenly Henry had an idea and lobbed the ball to him.

A gasp rose out of the stadium. Henry knew what everyone was thinking. It appeared that he was going to intentionally walk the lead-off man. Nothing like that had ever been done.

A moment later, the Met walked. Henry turned to the field and waved all the Cubs to the mound. They came in, frowning.

"Listen," Henry whispered when they were all there. "I don't have my arm anymore, but I do have a plan."

A moment later the players jogged back to their positions and Henry stared at the next batter. Out of the corner of his eye, he watched the runner on first start to take a lead. Henry spun and pretended to hurl the ball at first.

On first base, Stan Okie smacked his hand into his mitt to make a sound like a ball hitting. Then he tagged the runner out with the ball Henry had snuck to him during the huddle.

"Yer out!" the first-base umpire shouted.

"I didn't even see the ball!" the runner shouted.

"You know the kid throws fast," the umpire shouted back.

Henry smiled as the Met stormed back to his dugout. Okie threw him the ball and winked. One out, two to go. Once again, Henry walked the next Met intentionally. This time the batter stayed on the base and smiled knowingly at Henry.

"I dare you to run," Henry said.

The runner stopped smiling but stayed on the base.

"Double-dare you," Henry said.

"Just pitch the ball," the Met said.

"What's the matter?" Henry taunted him. "You chicken?" He tossed the ball into the air and then caught it. "See? You missed a golden opportunity there."

The runner shrugged. Henry tossed the ball even higher. "Chicken," he said and then made chicken noises. "*Bawk-bawk-bawk-bawk-bawk-bawk!*"

The other Cubs chuckled. Henry knew it had to be bothering the runner to have a twelve-year-old kid razzing him. Henry threw the ball even higher in the air and made more chicken noises. The runner stepped a little way off the bag.

"Quit it!" he shouted angrily at Henry. "Just pitch!"

But Henry just kept making chicken sounds and tossing the ball higher in the air. Finally he started to swing his arm as if he were going to throw it really high in the air.

Seeing that, the runner took a big lead off first.

Henry instantly stopped the swing and hurled the ball to first base, catching the runner off the bag. A second later the Met was caught in a rundown. The player was tagged out. The crowd exploded with cheers. Henry pumped his arm triumphantly. Two down, one to go.

But as Henry turned toward home plate, he saw a sight that made him stop and swallow with fear. Stepping up to the plate was his old nemesis, Alejandro Heddo.

Heddo grinned at him, revealing his gold teeth and reminding Henry of the first home run he ever gave up. Henry rubbed the ball nervously in his hands. What would he do now? Looking down in his mitt, he noticed that the tape with his name on it was starting to come off. Stalling for time, he pulled the tape off. Under it, scrawled in ink on the leather, was the name Mary.

Suddenly Henry realized whose glove it had been before. His mother's! She'd played ball! He looked up into the stands and caught her eye. She was motioning him to throw a floater.

Henry smiled and went into his windup. He leaned back and delivered . . . a floater!

The crowd went dead silent as the ball floated in a high arc through the air. Even Alejandro Heddo appeared captivated by the sight. At the last moment he remembered to swing. But it was too late! He missed.

"Strike one!" the umpire cried.

The crowd went bonkers! Frick threw the ball back. Henry went through the motions and threw . . . another floater!

This time Heddo was waiting for it. *Crack!* The ball rocketed down the left-field line. It was clearly going out of the ballpark. Henry covered his eyes, unable to watch.

"Foul!" the umpire shouted. "Strike two!"

Henry opened his eyes. The stadium was in bedlam! Heddo's hit had gone foul! The umpire threw out a new ball. Henry took off his mitt and started to rub it hard with both hands. The *have-to*, he thought. I gotta find it!

Meanwhile Heddo glowered at him. "You got nothing, kid! I know you got nothing!"

But Henry knew Heddo was wrong. He had the have-to! He started to laugh.

"What're you laughing at?" Heddo shouted at him.

"Nothing, sir!" Henry replied. He went into his pitching motion. It looked as if he was going to throw another floater. Heddo got ready for it.

Henry rocked and released . . . a flat one!

Heddo knew he'd been fooled. He tried to recover in time to swing. He swung, but he was off balance and missed.

"Strike three!" the umpire shouted.

The stadium erupted in cheers. The next thing Henry knew, he was surrounded by Cubs. They hoisted him onto their shoulders and paraded him around the field. Fans poured onto the field. People were doing cartwheels and somersaults. Photographers pressed toward Henry, and reporters tried to ask him questions. Henry was a hero. Thanks to him, the Cubs had won the division title!

In the locker room his teammates poured champagne on his head. The Cubs were really pumped. They were certain they could go on to win the league championship and the World Series, and begged Henry to change his mind and keep pitching. But Henry insisted this was his last game. They'd have to go the rest of the way without him. But he knew they could do it.

# epilogue

The next spring Henry played right field for the Oak Park Pirates again. The team was pretty much the same as it had been the year before, except Mrs. Rowengartner was now the coach, and Chet was the assistant coach. Henry was just like any other Little Leaguer. There was just one small difference — on the ring finger of his left hand he wore a gold ring with a blue stone. Inscribed in the ring was:

CHICAGO CUBS — WORLD CHAMPIONS.

The Cubs had won the Series!

## About the Author

Todd Strasser has written many award-winning novels for young and teenage readers. In addition, he frequently visits elementary and middle schools to speak about writing and conduct writing workshops. He played second base in Little League and hit one home run during his entire baseball career.